Futility: Or The Wreck of the Titan

Morgan Robertson

Futility: Or, The Wreck of the Titan

Table of Contents

Futility: Or, The Wreck of the Titan

Morgan Robertson

Chapter One

SHE was the largest craft afloat and the greatest of the works of men. In her construction and maintenance were involved every science, profession, and trade known to civilization. On her bridge were officers, who, besides being the pick of the Royal Navy, had passed rigid examinations in all studies that pertained to the winds, tides, currents, and geography of the sea; they were not only seamen, but scientists. The same professional standard applied to the personnel of the engine–room, and the steward's department was equal to that of a first–class hotel.

Two brass bands, two orchestras, and a theatrical company entertained the passengers during waking hours; a corps of physicians attended to the temporal, and a corps of chaplains to the spiritual, welfare of all on board, while a well–drilled fire–company soothed the fears of nervous ones and added to the general entertainment by daily practice with their apparatus.

From her lofty bridge ran hidden telegraph lines to the bow, stern engine–room, crow's–nest on the foremast, and to all parts of the ship where work was done, each wire terminating in a marked dial with a movable indicator, containing in its scope every order and answer required in handling the massive hulk, either at the dock or at sea —–which eliminated, to a great extent, the hoarse, nerve–racking shouts of officers and sailors.

From the bridge, engine–room, and a dozen places on her deck the ninety–two doors of nineteen water–tight compartments could be closed in half a minute by turning a lever. These doors would also close automatically in the presence of water. With nine compartments flooded the ship would still float, and so no known accident of the sea could possibly fill this many, the steamship Titan was considered practically unsinkable.

Built of steel throughout, and for passenger traffic only, she carried no combustible cargo to threaten her destruction by fire; and the immunity from the demand for cargo space had enabled her designers to discard the flat, kettle–bottom of cargo boats and give her the sharp dead–rise —– or slant from the keel —– of a steam yacht, and this improved her behavior in a seaway. She was eight hundred feet long, of seventy thousand tons displacement, seventy–five thousand horse–power, and on her trial trip had steamed at a rate of twenty–five knots an hour over the bottom, in the face of unconsidered winds, tides, and currents. In short, she was a floating city —– containing within her steel walls all that tends to minimize the dangers and discomforts of the Atlantic voyage —– all that makes life enjoyable.

Unsinkable —– indestructible, she carried as few boats as would satisfy the laws. These, twenty–four in number, were securely covered and lashed down to their chocks on the upper deck, and if launched would hold five hundred people. She carried no useless, cumbersome life–rafts; but —– because the law required it —– each of the three thousand berths in the passengers', officers', and crew's quarters contained a cork jacket, while about twenty circular life–buoys were strewn along the rails.

In view of her absolute superiority to other craft, a rule of navigation thoroughly believed in by some captains, but not yet openly followed, was announced by the steamship company to apply to the Titan: She would steam at full speed in fog, storm, and sunshine, and on the Northern Lane Route, winter and summer, for the following good and substantial reasons: First, that if another craft should strike her, the force of the impact would be distributed over a larger area if the Titan had full headway, and the brunt of the damage would be borne by the other. Second, that if the Titan was the aggressor she would certainly destroy the other craft, even at half–speed, and perhaps damage her own bows; while at full speed, she would cut her in two with no more damage to herself than a paintbrush could remedy. In either case, as the lesser of two evils, it was best that the smaller hull should suffer. A third reason was that, at full speed, she could be more easily steered out of danger, and a fourth, that in case of an end–on collision with an iceberg —– the only thing afloat that she could not conquer —– her bows would be crushed in but a few feet further at full than at half speed, and at the most three compartments would be flooded —– which would not matter with six more to spare.

So, it was confidently expected that when her engines had limbered themselves, the steamship Titan would land her passengers three thousand miles away with the promptitude and regularity of a railway train. She had beaten all records on her maiden voyage, but, up to the third return trip, had not lowered the time between Sandy Hook and Daunt's Rock to the five–day limit; and it was unofficially rumored among the two thousand passengers who had embarked at New York that an effort would now be made to do so.

Chapter Two

EIGHT tugs dragged the great mass to midstream and pointed her nose down the river; then the pilot on the bridge spoke a word or two; the first officer blew a short blast on the whistle and turned a lever; the tugs gathered in their lines and drew off; down in the bowels of the ship three small engines were started, opening the throttles of three large ones; three propellers began to revolve; and the mammoth, with a vibratory tremble running through her great frame, moved slowly to sea.

Futility: Or, The Wreck of the Titan

East of Sandy Hook the pilot was dropped and the real voyage begun. Fifty feet below her deck, in an inferno of noise, and heat, and light, and shadow, coal–passers wheeled the picked fuel from the bunkers to the fire–hold, where half–naked stokers, with faces like those of tortured fiends, tossed it into the eighty white–hot mouths of the furnaces. In the engine–room, oilers passed to and fro, in and out of the plunging, twisting, glistening steel, with oil–cans and waste, overseen by the watchful staff on duty, who listened with strained bearing for a false note in the confused jumble of sound —– a clicking of steel out of tune, which would indicate a loosened key or nut. On deck, sailors set the triangular sails on the two masts, to add their propulsion to the momentum of the record–breaker, and the passengers dispersed themselves as suited their several tastes. Some were seated in steamer cbairs, well wrapped —– for, though it was April, the salt air was chilly —– some paced the deck, acquiring their sea legs; others listened to the orchestra in the music–room, or read or wrote in the library, and a few took to their berths —– seasick from the slight heave of the ship on the ground–swell.

The decks were cleared, watches set at noon, and then began the never–ending cleaning–up at which steamship sailors put in so much of their time. Headed by a six–foot boatswain, a gang came aft on the starboard side, with, paint–buckets and brushes, and distributed themselves along the rail.

"Davits an' stanchions, men —– never mind the rail," said the boatswain. " Ladies, better move your chairs back a little. Rowland, climb down out o' that —– you'll be overboard. Take a ventilator —– no, you'll spill paint —– put your bucket away an' get some sandpaper from the yeoman. Work inboard till you get it out o' you."

The sailor addressed —– a slight–built man of about thirty, black–bearded and bronzed to the semblance of healthy vigor, but watery–eyed and unsteady of movement —– came down from the rail and shambled forward with his bucket. As he reached the group of ladies to whom the boatswain had spoken, his gaze rested on one —– a sunny–haired young woman with the blue of the sea in her eyes —– who had arisen at his approach. He started, turned aside as if to avoid her, and raising his hand in an embarrassed half–salute, passed on. Out of the boatswain's sight he leaned against the deck–house and panted, while he held his hand to his breast.

"What is it?" he muttered, wearily; "whisky nerves, or the dying flutter of a starved love. Five years, now —– and a look from her eyes can stop the blood in my veins —– can

4

bring back all the heart–hunger and helplessness, that leads a man to insanity —— or this." He looked at his trembling hand, all scarred and tar–stained, passed on forward, and returned with the sandpaper.

The young woman had been equally affected by the meeting. An expression of mingled surprise and terror had come to her pretty, but rather weak face; and without acknowledging his half–salute, she had caught up a little child from the deck behind her, and turning into the saloon door, hurried to the library, where she sank into a chair beside a military–looking gentleman, who glanced up from a book and remarked: "Seen the sea–serpent, Myra, or the Flying Dutchman? What's up?"

"Oh, George —— no," she answered in agitated tones. "John Rowland is here —— Lieutenant Rowland. I've just seen him —— he is so changed —— he tried to speak to me."

"Who —— that troublesome flame of yours? I never met him, you know, and you haven't told me much about him. What is he —— first cabin?"

" No, he seems to be a common sailor; he is working, and is dressed in old clothes —— all dirty. And such a dissipated face, too. He seems to have fallen —— so low. And it is all since ——"

"Since you soured on him? Well, it is no fault of yours, dear. If a man has it in him he'll go to the dogs anyhow. How is his sense of injury? Has he a grievance or a grudge? You're badly upset. What did he say?"

"I don't know —— he said nothing —— I've always been afraid of him. I've met him three times since then, and he puts such a frightful look in his eyes —— and he was so violent, and headstrong, and so terribly angry, —— that time. He accused me of leading him on, and playing with him; and he said something about an immutable law of chance, and a governing balance of events —— that I couldn't understand, only where he said that for all the suffering we inflict on others, we receive an equal amount ourselves. Then he went away —— in such a passion. I've imagined ever since that he would take some revenge —— he might steal our Myra —— our baby." She strained the smiling child to her breast and went on. "I liked him at first, until I found out that he was an atheist —— why, George, he actually denied the existence of God —— and to me, a professing Christian."

5

"He had a wonderful nerve," said the husband, with a smile; "didn't know you very well, I should say."

"He never seemed the same to me after that," she resumed; "I felt as though in the presence of something unclean. Yet I thought how glorious it would be if I could save him to God, and tried to convince him of the loving care of Jesus; but he only ridiculed all I hold sacred, and said, that much as he valued my good opinion, he would not be a hypocrite to gain it, and that he would be honest with himself and others, and express his honest unbelief —— the idea; as though one could be honest without God's help —— and then, one day, I smelled liquor on his breath —— he always smelled of tobacco —— and I gave him up. It was then that he that he broke out."

"Come out and show me this reprobate," said the husband, rising. They went to the door and the young woman peered out. "He is the last man down there —– close to the cabin," she said as she drew in. The husband stepped out.

"What! that hang–dog ruffian, scouring the ventilator? So, that's Rowland, of the navy, is it! Well, this is a tumble. Wasn't he broken for conduct unbecoming an officer? Got roaring drunk at the President's levee, didn't he? I think I read of it."

"I know he lost his position and was terribly disgraced," answered the wife.

"Well, Myra, the poor devil is harmless now. We'll be across in a few days, and you needn't meet him on this broad deck. If he hasn't lost all sensibility, he's as embarrassed as you. Better stay in now —– it's getting foggy."

Chapter Three

WHEN the watch turned out at midnight, they found a vicious half–gale blowing from the northeast, which, added to the speed of the steamship, made, so far as effects on her deck went, a fairly uncomfortable whole gale of chilly wind. The head sea, choppy as compared with her great length, dealt the Titan successive blows, each one attended by supplementary tremors to the continuous vibrations of the engines —— each one sending a cloud of thick spray aloft that reached the crow's–nest on the foremast and battered the pilot–house windows on the bridge in a liquid bombardment that would have broken ordinary glass. A fog–bank, into which the ship had plunged in the afternoon, still enveloped her —— damp and impenetrable; and into the gray, ever–receding wall ahead, with two deck officers and three lookouts straining sight and hearing to the utmost, the great racer was charging with undiminished speed.

At a quarter past twelve, two men crawled in from the darkness at the ends of the eighty–foot bridge and shouted to the first officer, who had just taken the deck, the names of the men who had relieved them. Backing up to the pilot–house, the officer repeated the names to a quartermaster within, who entered them in the log–book. Then the men vanisbed —– to their coffee and "watch–below." In a few moments another dripping shape appeared on the bridge and reported the crow's–nest relief.

"Rowland, you say?" bawled the officer above the howling of the wind." Is he the man who was lifted aboard, drunk, yesterday?"

"Yes, sir."

"Is he still drunk?"

"Yes, sir."

"All right —– that'll do. Enter Rowland in the crow's–nest, quartermaster," said the officer; then, making a funnel of his hands, he roared out: "Crow's–nest, there."

"Sir," came the answer, shrill and clear on the gale.

"Keep your eyes open —– keep a sharp lookout."

"Very good, sir."

"Been a man–o'–war's–man, I judge, by his answer. They're no good," muttered the officer. He resumed his position at the forward side of the bridge where the wooden railing afforded some shelter from the raw wind, and began the long vigil which would only end when the second officer relieved him, four hours later. Conversation —– except in the line of duty —– was forbidden among the bridge officers of the Titan, and his watchmate, the third officer, stood on the other side of the large bridge binnacle, only leaving this position occasionally to glance in at the compass —— which seemed to be his sole duty at sea. Sheltered by one of the deck-houses below, the boatswain and the watch paced back and forth, enjoying the only two hours respite which steamship rules afforded, for the day's work had ended with the going down of the other watch, and at two o'clock the washing of the 'tween-deck would begin, as an opening task in the next day's labor.

By the time one bell had sounded, with its repetition from the crow's-nest, followed by a long-drawn cry —— "all's well" —— from the lookouts, the last of the two thousand passengers had retired, leaving the spacious cabins and steerage in possession of the watchmen; while, sound asleep in his cabin abaft the chart-room was the captain, the commander who never commanded —— unless the ship was in danger; for the pilot had charge, making and leaving port, and the officers, at sea.

Two bells were struck and answered; then three, and the boatswain and his men were lighting up for a final smoke, when there rang out overhead a startling cry from the crow's-nest:

"Something ahead, sir —— can't make it out."

The first officer sprang to the engine-room telegraph and grasped the lever. "Sing out what you see," he roared.

Hard aport, sir —— ship on the starboard tack —— dead ahead" came the cry.

"Port your wheel —— hard over," repeated the first officer to the quartermaster at the helm —— who answered and obeyed. Nothing as yet could be seen from the bridge. The powerful steering-engine in the stern ground the rudder over; but before three degrees on the compass card were traversed by the lubber's-point, a seeming thickening of the darkness and fog ahead resolved itself into the square sails of a deep-laden ship, crossing the Titan's bow, not half her length away.

"H—l and d——" growled the first officer. Steady on your course, quartermaster," he shouted. "Stand from under on deck." He turned a lever which closed compartments, pushed a button marked —— "Captain's Room," and crouched down, awaiting the crash.

There was hardly a crash. A slight jar shook the forward end of the Titan and sliding down her foretopmast–stay and rattling on deck came a shower of small spars, sails, blocks, and wire rope. Then, in the darkness to starboard and port, two darker shapes shot by —– the two halves of the ship she had cut through; and from one of these shapes, where still burned a binnacle light, was heard, high above the confused murmur of shouts and shrieks, a sailorly voice:

"May the curse of God light on you and your cheese–knife, you brass–bound murderers."

The shapes were swallowed in the blackness astern; the cries were hushed by the clamor of the gale, and the steamship Titan swung back to her course. The first officer had not turned the lever of the engineroom telegraph.

The boatswain bounded up the steps of the bridge for instructions.

"Put men at the batches and doors. Send every one who comes on deck to the chart–room. Tell the watchman to notice what the passengers have learned, and clear away that wreck forward as soon as possible." The voice of the officer was hoarse and strained as he gave these directions, and the " aye, aye, sir" of the boatswain was uttered in a gasp.

Chapter Four

HE crow's–nest "lookout," sixty feet above the deck, had seen every detail of the horror, from the moment when the upper sails of the doomed ship had appeared to him above the fog to the time when the last tangle of wreckage was cut away by his watchmates below. When relieved at four bells, he descended with as little strength in his limbs as was compatible with safety in the rigging. At the rail, the boatswain met him.

"Report your relief, Rowland," he said, "and go into the chart–room!"

On the bridge, as he gave the name of his successor, the first officer seized his hand, pressed it, and repeated the boatswain's order. In the chart–room, he found the captain of the Titan, pale–faced and intense in manner, seated at a table, and, grouped around him, the whole of the watch on deck except the officers, lookouts, and quartermasters. The cabin watchmen were there, and some of the watch below, among whom were stokers and coal—passers, and also, a few of the idlers–lampmen, yeomen, and butchers, who, sleeping forward, had been awakened by the terrific blow of the great hollow knife within which they lived.

Three carpenters' mates stood by the door, with sounding–rods in their hands, which they had just shown the captain —— dry. Every face, from the captain's down, wore a look of horror and expectancy. A quartermaster followed Rowland in and said:

"Engineer felt no jar in the engine–room, sir; and there's no excitement in the stokehold."

"And you watchmen report no alarm in the cabins. How about the steerage? Is that man back?" asked the captain. Another watchman appeared as he spoke.

"All asleep in the steerage, sir," he said. Then a quartermaster entered with the same report of the forecastles.

"Very well," said the captain, rising; "one by one come into my office —— watchmen first, then petty officers, then the men. Quartermasters will watch the door —— that no man goes out until I have seen him." He passed into another room, followed by a watchman, who presently emerged and went on deck with a more pleasant expression of face. Another entered and came out; then another, and another, until every man but Rowland had been within the sacred precincts, all to wear the same pleased, or satisfied, look on reappearing. When Rowland entered, the captain, seated at a desk, motioned him to a chair, and asked his name.

"John Rowland," he answered. The captain wrote it down.

"I understand," he said, "that you were in the crow's–nest when this unfortunate collision occurred."

"Yes, sir; and I reported the ship as soon as I saw her."

"You are not here to be censured. You are aware, of course, that nothing could be done, either to avert this terrible calamity, or to save life afterward."

"Nothing at a speed of twenty–five knots an hour in a thick fog, sir." The captain glanced sharply at Rowland and frowned.

"We will not discuss the speed of the ship, my good man," he said, " or the rules of the company. You will find, when you are paid at Liverpool, a package addressed to you at the company's office containing one hundred pounds in banknotes. This, you will receive for your silence in regard to this collision —– the reporting of which would embarrass the company and help no one."

"On the contrary, captain, I shall not receive it. On the contrary, sir, I shall speak of this wholesale murder at the first opportunity!"

The captain leaned back and stared at the debauched face, the trembling figure of the sailor, with which this defiant speech so little accorded. Under ordinary circumstances, he would have sent him on deck to be dealt with by the officers. But this was not an ordinary circumstance. In the watery eyes was a look of shock, and horror, and honest indignation; the accents were those of an educated man; and the consequences hanging over himself and the company for which he worked —– already complicated by and involved in his efforts to avoid them —– which this man might precipitate, were so extreme, that such questions as insolence and difference in rank were not to be thought of. He must meet and subdue this Tartar on common ground —– as man to man.

"Are you aware, Rowland," he asked, quietly, "that you will stand alone —– that you will be discredited, lose your berth, and make enemies?"

"I am aware of more than that," answered Rowland, excitedly. "I know of the power vested in you as captain. I know that you can order me into irons from this room for any offense you wish to imagine. And I know that an unwitnessed, uncorroborated entry in your official log concerning me would be evidence enough to bring me life imprisonment. But I also know something of admiralty law; that from my prison cell I can send you and your first officer to the gallows."

"You are mistaken in your conceptions of evidence. I could not cause your conviction by a log–book entry; nor could you, from a prison, injure me. What are you, may I ask —– an ex–lawyer?"

Futility: Or, The Wreck of the Titan

"A graduate of Annapolis. Your equal in professional technic."

"And you have interest at Washington?"

"None whatever."

"And what is your object in taking this stand —– which can do you no possible good, though certainly not the harm you speak of?"

"That I may do one good, strong act in my useless life —– that I may help to arouse such a sentiment of anger in the two countries as will forever end this wanton destruction of life and property for the sake of speed–that will save the hundreds of fishing–craft, and others, run down yearly, to their owners, and the crews to their families."

Both men had risen and the captain was pacing the floor as Rowland, with flashing eyes and clinched fists, delivered this declaration.

"A result to be hoped for, Rowland," said the former, pausing before him, "but beyond your power or mine to accomplish. Is the amount I named large enough? Could you fill a position on my bridge? "

"I can fill a higher; and your company is not rich enough to buy me."

"You seem to be a man without ambition; but you must have wants."

"Food, clothing, shelter–and whisky," said Rowland with a bitter, self–contemptuous laugh. The captain reached down a decanter and two glasses from a swinging tray and said as he placed them before him:

"Here is one of your wants; fill up." Rowland's eyes glistened as he poured out a glassful, and the captain followed.

"I will drink with you, Rowland," he said; "here is to our better understanding." He tossed off the liquor; then Rowland, who had waited, said: "I prefer drinking alone, captain," and drank the whisky at a gulp. The captain's face flushed at the affront, but he controlled himself.

"Go on deck, now, Rowland," he said; "I will talk with you again before we reach soundings. Meanwhile, I request —– not require, but request —– that you hold no useless conversation with your shipmates in regard to this matter."

To this first officer, when relieved at eight bells, the captain said: "He is a broken–down wreck with a temporarily active conscience; but is not the man to buy or intimidate: he knows too much. However, we've found his weak point. If he gets snakes before we dock, his testimony is worthless. Fill him up and I'll see the surgeon, and study up on drugs."

When Rowland turned out to breakfast at seven bells that morning, he found a pint flask in the pocket of his pea–jacket, which he felt of but did not pull out in sight of his watchmates.

"Well, captain," he thought, "you are, in truth, about as puerile, insipid a scoundrel as ever escaped the law. I'll save you your drugged Dutch courage for evidence." But it was not drugged, as he learned later. It was good whisky —– a leader —– to warm his stomach while the captain was studying.

Chapter Five

N incident occurred that morning which drew Rowland's thoughts far from the happenings of the night. A few hours of bright sunshine had brought the passengers on deck like bees from a hive, and the two broad promenades resembled, in color and life, the streets of a city. The watch was busy at the inevitable scrubbing, and Rowland, with a swab and bucket, was cleaning the white paint on the starboard taffrail, screened from view by the after deck–house, which shut off a narrow space at the stern. A little girl ran into the enclosure, laughing and screaming, and clung to his legs, while she jumped up and down in an overflow of spirits.

"I wunned 'way," she said; "I wunned 'way from mamma."

Drying his wet bands on his trousers, Rowland lifted the tot and said, tenderly: "Well, little one, you must run back to mamma. You're in bad company." The innocent eyes smiled into his own, and then —– a foolish proceeding, which only bachelors are guilty of —– he held her above the rail in jesting menace. "Shall I drop you over to the fishes, baby?" he asked, while his features softened to an unwonted smile. The child gave a little scream of fright, and at that instant a young woman appeared around the corner. She sprang toward Rowland like a tigress, snatched the child, stared at him for a moment with dilated eyes, and then disappeared, leaving him limp and nerveless, breathing hard.

"It is her child," he groaned. "That was the mother–look. She is married —– married." He resumed his work, with a face as near the color of the paint he was scrubbing as the tanned skin of a sailor may become.

Ten minutes later, the captain, in his office, was listening to a complaint from a very excited man and woman.

"And you say, colonel," said the captain, "that this man Rowland is an old enemy?"

"He is —– or was once —– a rejected admirer of Mrs. Selfridge. That is all I know of him —– except that he has hinted at revenge. My wife is certain of what she saw, and I think the man should be confined."

"Why, captain," said the woman, vehemently, as she bugged her child, "you should have seen him; he was just about to drop Myra over as I seized her —– and he had such a frightful leer on his face, too. Oh, it was hideous. I shall not sleep another wink in this ship —–I know."

"I beg you will give yourself no uneasiness, madam," said the captain, gravely. "I have already learned something of his antecedents —– that he is a disgraced and broken–down naval officer; but, as he has sailed three voyages with us, I had credited his willingness to work before–the–mast to his craving for liquor, which he could not satisfy without money. However —– as you think —– he may be following you. Was he able to learn of your movements —– that you were to take passage in this ship?"

"Why not?" exclaimed the husband; "he must know some of Mrs. Selfridge's friends."

"Yes, yes," she said, eagerly; "I have heard him spoken of, several times."

"Then it is clear," said the captain. "If you will agree, madam, to testify against him in the English courts, I will immediately put him in irons for attempted murder."

"Oh, do, captain," she exclaimed. "I cannot feel safe while he is at liberty. Of course I will testify."

"Whatever you do, captain," said the husband, savagely, "rest assured that I shall put a bullet through his head if he meddles with me or mine again. Then you can put me in irons."

"I will see that he is attended to, colonel," replied the captain as he bowed them out of his office.

But, as a murder charge is not always the best way to discredit a man; and as the captain did not believe that the man who had defied him would murder a child; and as the charge would be difficult to prove in any case, and would cause him much trouble and annoyance, he did not order the arrest of John Rowland, but merely directed that, for the time, he should be kept at work by day in the 'tween–deck, out of sight of the passengers.

Rowland, surprised at his sudden transfer from the disagreeable scrubbing to a "soldier's job" of painting life–buoys in the warm 'tween–deck, was shrewd enough to know that he was being closely watched by the boatswain that morning, but not shrewd enough to affect any symptoms of intoxication or drugging, which might have satisfied his anxious superiors and brought him more whisky. As a result of his brighter eyes and steadier voice —– due to the curative sea air —– when he turned out for the first dog–watch on deck at four o'clock, the captain and boatswain held an interview in the chart–room, in which the former said: "Do not be alarmed. It is not poison. He is half–way into the horrors now, and this will merely bring them on. He will see snakes, ghosts, goblins, shipwrecks, fire, and all sorts of things. It works in two or three hours. Just drop it into his drinking pot while the port forecastle is empty."

There was a fight in the port forecastle—–to which Rowland belonged —– at supper–time, which need not be described beyond mention of the fact that Rowland, who was not a participant, had his pot of tea dashed from his hand before he had taken three swallows. He procured a fresh supply and finished his supper; then, taking no part in his watchmates' open discussion of the fight, and guarded discussion of collisions, rolled into his bunk and smoked until eight bells, when he turned out with the rest.

Chapter Six

ROWLAND," said the big boatswain, as the watch mustered on deck; "take the starboard bridge lookout."

"It is not my trick, boats'n," said Rowland, in surprise.

"Orders from the bridge. Get up there."

Rowland grumbled, as sailors may when aggrieved, and obeyed. The man he relieved reported his name, and disappeared; the first officer sauntered down the bridge, uttered the official, "keep a good lookout," and returned to his post; then the silence and loneliness of a night–watch at sea, intensified by the never–ceasing hum of the engines, and relieved only by the sounds of distant music and laughter from the theater, descended on the forward part of the ship. For the fresh westerly wind, coming with the Titan, made nearly a calm on her deck; and the dense fog, though overshone by a bright star–specked sky, was so chilly that the last talkative passenger had fled to the light and life within.

When three bells —– half–past, nine —– had sounded, and Rowland had given in his turn the required call —– "all's well" —– the first officer left his post and approached him.

"Rowland," he said as he drew near; "I hear you've walked the quarter–deck."

"I cannot imagine how you learned it, sir," replied Rowland; "I am not in the babit of referring to it."

"You told the captain. I suppose the curriculum is as complete at Annapolis as at the Royal Naval College. What do you think of Maury's theories of currents?"

"They seem plausible," said Rowland, unconsciously dropping the "sir"; "but I think that in most particulars he has been proven wrong."

"Yes, I think so myself. Did you ever follow up another idea of his —– that of locating the position of ice in a fog by the rate of decrease in temperature as approached? "

"Not to any definite result. But it seems to be only a matter of calculation, and time to calculate. Cold is negative heat, and can be treated like radiant energy, decreasing as the square of the distance."

The officer stood a moment, looking ahead and humming a tune to himself; then, saying: "Yes, that s so," returned to his place.

"Must have a cast–iron stomach," he muttered, as he peered into the binnacle; "or else the boats'n dosed the wrong man's pot."

Rowland glanced after the retreating officer with a cynical smile. "I wonder," he said to himself, "why he comes down here talking navigation to a foremast hand. Why am I up here —– out of my turn? Is this something in line with that bottle? "He resumed the short pacing back and forth on the end of the bridge, and the rather gloomy train of thought which the officer had interrupted. "How long," he mused, "would his ambition and love of profession last him after he had met, and won, and lost, the only woman on earth to him? Why is it —– that failure to hold the affections of one among the millions of women who live, and love, can outweigh every blessing in life, and turn a man's nature into a hell, to consume him? Who did she marry? Some one, probably a stranger long after my banishment, who came to her possessed of a few qualities of mind or physique that pleased her, —– who did not need to love her —– his chances were better without that —– and he steps coolly and easily into my heaven. And they tell us, that 'God doeth all things well,' and that there is a heaven where all our unsatisfied wants are attended to —– provided we have the necessary faith in it. That means, if it means anything, that after a lifetime of unrecognized allegiance, during which I win nothing but her fear and contempt, I may be rewarded by the love and companionship of her soul. Do I love her soul? Has her soul beauty of face and the figure and carriage of a Venus? Has her soul deep, blue eyes and a sweet, musical voice. Has it wit, and grace, and charm? Has it a wealth of pity for suffering? These are the things I loved. I do not love her soul, if she has one. I do not want it. I want her —– I need her." He stopped in his walk and leaned against the bridge railing, with eyes fixed on the fog ahead. He was speaking his thoughts aloud now, and the first officer drew within bearing, listened a moment, and went back. "Working on him," he whispered to the third officer. Then he pushed the button which called the captain, blew a short blast of the steam whistle as a call to the boatswain, and resumed his watch on the drugged lookout, while the third officer conned the ship.

The steam call to the boatswain is so common a sound on a steamship as to generally pass unnoticed. This call affected another besides the boatswain. A little night−gowned figure arose from an under berth in a saloon stateroom, and, with wide−open, staring eyes, groped its way to the deck, unobserved by the watchman. The white, bare little feet felt no cold as they pattered the planks of the deserted promenade, and the little figure had reached the steerage entrance by the time the captain and boatswain had reached the bridge.

"And they talk," went on Rowland, as the three watched and listened; "of the wonderful love and care of a merciful God, who controls all things —− who has given me my defects, and my capacity for loving, and then placed Myra Gaunt in my way. Is there mercy to me in this? As part of a great evolutionary principle, which develops the race life at the expense of the individual, it might be consistent with the idea of a God —− a first cause. But does the individual who perishes, because unfitted to survive, owe any love, or gratitude to this God? He does not! On the supposition that He exists, I deny it! And on the complete lack of evidence that He does exist, I affirm to myself the integrity of cause and effect —− which is enough to explain the Universe, and me. A merciful God —− a kind, loving, just, and merciful God —−" he burst into a fit of incongruous laughter, which stopped short as he clapped his hands to his stomach and then to his head. "What ails me?" he gasped; "I feel as though I had swallowed hot coals —− and my head —− and my eyes —− I can't see." The pain left him in a moment and the laughter returned. "What's wrong with the starboard anchor? It's moving. It's changing It's a —− what? What on earth is it? On end —− and the windlass —− and the spare anchors —− and the davits —− all alive —− all moving."

The sight he saw would have been horrid to a healthy mind, but it only moved this man to increased and uncontrollable merriment. The two rails below leading to the stern had arisen before him in a shadowy triangle; and within it were the deck−fittings he had mentioned. The windlass had become a thing of horror, black and forbidding. The two end barrels were the bulging, lightless eyes of a non−descript monster, for which the cable chains had multiplied themselves into innumerable legs and tentacles. And this thing was crawling around within the triangle. The anchor−davits were many−headed serpents which danced on their tails, and the anchors themselves writhed and squirmed in

18

the shape of immense hairy caterpillars, while faces appeared on the two white lantern–towers —– grinning and leering at him. With his hands on the bridge rail, and tears streaming down his face, he laughed at the strange sight, but did not speak; and the three, who had quietly approached, drew back to await, while below on the promenade deck, the little white figure, as though attracted by his laughter, turned into the stairway leading to the upper deck.

The phantasmagoria faded to a blank wall of gray fog, and Rowland found sanity to mutter, "They've drugged me"; but in an instant he stood in the darkness of a garden —– one that he had known. In the distance were the lights of a house, and close to him was a young girl, who turned from him and fled, even as he called to her.

By a supreme effort of will, he brought himself back to the present, to the bridge stood upon, and to his duty. "Why must it haunt me through the years," he groaned; "drunk then —– drunk since. She could have saved me, but she chose to damn me." He strove to pace up and down, but staggered, and clung to the rail; while the three watchers approached again, and the little white figure below climbed the upper bridge steps.

The survival of the fittest," he rambled, as he stared into the fog; "cause and effect. It explains the Universe —– and me." He lifted his hand and spoke loudly, as though to some unseen familiar of the deep. What will be the last effect? Where in the scheme of ultimate balance —– under the law of the correlation of energy, will my wasted wealth of love be gathered, and weighed, and credited? What will balance it, and where will I be? Myra, —– Myra," he called; "do you know what you have lost? Do you know, in your goodness, and purity, and truth, of what you have done? Do you know —–"

The fabric on which he stood was gone, and he seemed to be poised on nothing in a worldless universe of gray–alone. And in the vast, limitless emptiness there was no sound, or life, or change; and in his heart neither fear, nor wonder, nor emotion of any kind, save one —– the unspeakable hunger of a love that had failed. Yet it seemed that he was not John Rowland, but some one, or something else; for presently he saw himself, far away —– millions of billions of miles; as though on the outermost fringes of the void —– and beard his own voice, calling. Faintly, yet distinctly, filled with the concentrated despair of his life, came the call: "Myra, —– Myra."

19

There was an answering call, and looking for the second voice, he beheld her —– the woman of his love —– on the opposite edge of space; and her eyes held the tenderness, and her voice held the pleading that he had known but in dreams. "Come back," she called; "come back to me." But it seemed that the two could not understand; for again he heard the despairing cry: "Myra, Myra, where are you?" and again the answer: "Come back. Come."

Then in the far distance to the right appeared a faint point of flame, which grew larger. It was approacbing, and he dispassionately viewed it; and when he looked again for the two, they were gone, and in their places were two clouds of nebula, which resolved into myriad points of sparkling light and color —– whirling, encroaching, until they filled all space. And through them the larger light was coming —– and growing larger —– straight for him.

He heard a rushing sound, and looking for it, saw in the opposite direction a formless object, as much darker than the gray of the void as the flame was brighter, and it too was growing larger, and coming. And it seemed to him that this light and darkness were the good and evil of his life, and he watched, to see which would reach him first, but felt no surprise or regret when he saw that the darkness was nearest. It came, closer and closer, until it brushed him on the side.

"What have we here, Rowland?" said a voice. Instantly, the whirling points were blotted out; the universe of gray changed to the fog; the flame of light to the moon rising above it, and the shapeless darkness to the form of the first officer. The little white figure, which had just darted past the three watchers, stood at his feet. As though warned by an inner subconsciousness of danger, it had come in its sleep, for safety and care, to its mother's old lover —– the strong and the weak —– the degraded and disgraced, but exalted —– the persecuted, drugged, and all but helpless John Rowland.

With the readiness with which a man who dozes while standing will answer the question that wakens him, he said —– though he stammered from the now waning effect of the drug: "Myra's child, sir; it's asleep." He picked up the night–gowned little girl, who screamed as she wakened, and folded his pea–jacket around the cold little body.

"Who is Myra?" asked the officer in a bullying tone, in which were also chagrin and disappointment. "You've been asleep yourself."

Before Rowland could reply a shout from the crow's-nest split the air.

"Ice," yelled the lookout; "ice ahead. Iceberg. Right under the bows." The first officer ran amid-ships, and the captain, who had remained there, sprang to the engine-room telegraph, and this time the lever was turned. But in five seconds the bow of the Titan began to lift, and ahead, and on either hand, could be seen, through the fog, a field of ice, which arose in an incline to a hundred feet high in her track. The music in the theater ceased, and among the babel of shouts and cries, and the deafening noise of steel, scraping and crashing over ice, Rowland heard the agonized voice of a woman crying from the bridge steps: "Myra, — Myra, where are you? Come back."

Chapter Seven

SEVENTY-FIVE thousand tons — dead-weight — rushing through the fog at the rate of fifty feet a second, had hurled itself at an iceberg. Had the impact been received by a perpendicular wall the elastic resistance of bending plates and frames would have overcome the momentum with no more damage to the passengers than a severe shaking up, and to the ship than the crushing in of her bows and the killing, to a man, of the watch below. She would have backed off, and slightly down by the head, finished the voyage at reduced speed to rebuild on insurance money, and benefit, largely, in the end, by the consequent advertising of her indestructibility. But a low beach, possibly formed by the recent overturning of the berg, received the Titan, and with her keel cutting the ice like the steel runner of an iceboat, and her great weight resting on the starboard bilge, she rose out of the sea, higher and higher — until the propellers in the stern were half exposed — then, meeting an easy, spiral rise in the ice under her port bow, she heeled, overbalanced, and crashed down on her side, to starboard.

The holding-down bolts of twelve boilers and three triple-expansion engines, unintended to hold such weights from a perpendicular flooring, snapped, and down through a maze of ladders, gratings, and fore-and-aft bulkheads came these giant masses of steel and iron, puncturing the sides of the ship, even where backed by solid, resisting ice; and filling the engine and boiler-rooms with scalding steam, which brought a quick, though tortured death, to each of the hundred men on duty in the engineer's department.

Amid the roar of escaping steam, and the bee-like buzzing of nearly three thousand human voices, raised in agonized screams and callings from within the enclosing walls, and the whistling of air through hundreds of open dead–lights as the water, entering the holes of the crushed and riven starboard side, expelled it, the Titan moved slowly backward and launched herself into the sea, where she floated low on her side —– a dying monster, groaning with her death–wound.

A solid, pyramid–like hummock of ice, left to starboard as the steamer ascended, and which projected close alongside the upper, or boat–deck, as she fell over, had caught, in succession, every pair of davits to starboard, bending and wrenching them, smashing boats, and snapping tackles and gripes, until, as the ship cleared herself, it capped the pile of wreckage strewing the ice in front of, and around it, with the end and broken stanchions of the bridge. And in this shattered, box–like structure, dazed by the sweeping fall through an arc of seventy–foot radius, crouched Rowland, bleeding from a cut in his head, and still holding to his breast the little girl —– now too frightened to cry.

By an effort of will, he aroused himself and looked. To his eyesight, twisted and fixed to a shorter focus by, the drug he had taken, the steamship was little more than a bloth on the moon–whitened fog; yet he thought be could see men clambering and working on the upper davits, and the nearest boat —– No. 24 —– seemed to be swinging by the tackles. Then the fog shut her out, though her position was still indicated by the roaring of steam from her iron lungs. This ceased in time, leaving behind it the horrid humming sound and whistling of air; and when this too was suddenly hushed, and the ensuing silence broken by dull, booming reports —– as from bursting compartments —– Rowland knew that the holocaust was complete; that the invincible Titan, with nearly all of her people, unable to climb vertical floors and ceilings, was beneath the surface of the sea.

Mechanically, his benumbed faculties had received and recorded the impressions of the last few moments; he could not comprehend, to the full, the horror of it all. Yet his mind was keenly alive to the peril of the woman whose appealing voice he had heard and recognized —– tbe woman of his dream, and the mother of the child in his arms. He hastily examined the wreckage. Not a boat was intact. Creeping down to the water's edge, he hailed, with all the power of his weak voice, to possible, but invisible boats beyond the fog —– calling on them to come and save the child —– to look out for a woman who had been on deck, under the bridge. He shouted this woman's name —– the one that he knew —– encouraging her to swim, to tread water, to float on wreckage, and to answer him, until he came to her. There was no response, and when his voice had grown hoarse and futile, and his feet numb from the cold of the thawing ice, he returned to the wreckage, weighed down and all but crushed by the blackest desolation that had, so far, come into his unhappy life. The little girl was crying and he tried to soothe her.

"I want mamma," she wailed.

"Hush, baby, hush," he answered, wearily and bitterly; "so do I —— more than Heaven, but I think our chances are about even now. Are you cold, little one? We'll go inside, and I'll make a house for us."

He removed his coat, tenderly wrapped the little figure in it, and with the injunction: "Don't be afraid, now," placed her in the corner of the bridge, which rested on its forward side. As he did so, the bottle of whisky fell out of the pocket. It seemed an age since he had found it there, and it required a strong effort of reasoning before be remembered its full significance. Then he raised it, to hurl it down the incline of ice, but stopped himself.

"I'll keep it," he muttered; "it may be safe in small quantities, and we'll need it on this ice." He placed it in a corner; then, removing the canvas cover from one of the wrecked boats, he hung it over the open side and end of the bridge, crawled within, and donned his coat —— a ready–made, slop–cbest garment, designed for a larger man —— and buttoning it around himself and the little girl, lay down on the hard woodwork. She was still crying, but soon, under the influence of the warmth of his body, ceased and went to sleep.

Huddled in a corner, he gave himself up to the torment of his thoughts. Two pictures alternately crowded his mind; one, that of the woman of his dream, entreating him to come back —— which his memory clung to as an oracle; the other, of this woman, cold and lifeless, fathoms deep in the sea. He pondered on her chances. She was close to, or on the bridge steps; and boat No. 24, which he was almost sure was being cleared away as he looked, would swing close to her as it descended. She could climb in and be saved —— unless the swimmers from doors and hatches should swamp the boat. And, in his agony of mind, he cursed these swimmers, preferring to see her, mentally, the only passenger in the boat, with the watch–on–deck to pull her to safety.

The potent drug he had taken was still at work, and this, with the musical wash of the sea on the icy beach, and the muffled creaking and crackling beneath and around him —— tbe voice of the iceberg —— overcame him finally, and he slept, to waken at daylight with limbs stiffened and numb —– almost frozen.

And all night, as he slept, a boat with the number twenty–four on her bow, pulled by sturdy sailors and steered by brass–buttoned officers, was making for the Southern Lane —– tbe highway of spring traffic. And, crouched in the stern–sheets of this boat was a moaning, praying woman, who cried and screamed at intervals, for husband and baby, and would not be comforted, even when one of the brass–buttoned officers assured her that her child was safe in the care of John Rowland, a brave and trusty sailor, who was certainly in the other boat with it. He did not tell her, of course, that Rowland had hailed from the berg as she lay unconscious, and that if he still had the child, it was with him there —– deserted.

Chapter Eight

ROWLAND, with some misgivings, drank a small quantity of the liquor, and wrapping the still sleeping child in the coat, stepped out on the ice. The fog was gone and a blue, sailless sea stretched out to the horizon. Behind him was ice —– a mountain of it. He climbed the elevation and looked at another stretch of vacant view from a precipice a hundred feet high. To his left the ice sloped to a steeper beach than the one behind him, and to the right, a pile of hummocks and taller peaks, interspersed with numerous caons and caves, and glistening with waterfalls, shut out the horizon in this direction. Nowhere was there a sail or steamer's smoke to cheer him, and he retraced his steps. When but half–way to the wreckage, he saw a moving white object approaching from the direction of the peaks.

His eyes were not yet in good condition, and after an uncertain scrutiny he started at a run; for he saw that the mysterious white object was nearer the bridge than himself, and rapidly lessening the distance. A hundred yards away, his heart bounded and the blood in his veins felt cold as the ice under foot, for the white object proved to be a traveler from the frozen North, lean and famished —– a polar bear, who had scented food and was seeking it —– coming on at a lumbering run, with great red jaws half open and yellow fangs exposed. Rowland had no weapon but a strong jackknife, but this he pulled from his pocket and opened as he ran. Not for an instant did be hesitate at a conflict that promised almost certain death; for the presence of this bear involved the safety of a child whose life had become of more importance to him than his own. To his horror, he saw it creep out of the opening in its white covering, just as the bear turned the corner of the bridge.

"Go back, baby, go back," he shouted, as he bounded down the slope. The bear reached the child first, and with seemingly no effort, dashed it, with a blow of its massive paw, a dozen feet away, where it lay quiet. Turning to follow, the brute was met by Rowland.

The bear rose to his haunches, sank down, and charged; and Rowland felt the bones of his left arm crushing under the bite of the big, yellow-fanged jaws. But, falling, he buried the knife-blade in the shaggy hide, and the bear, with an angry snarl, spat out the mangled member and dealt him a sweeping blow which sent him farther along the ice than the child had gone. He arose, with broken ribs, and —– scarcely feeling the pain —– awaited the second charge. Again was the crushed and useless arm gripped in the yellow vise, and again was he pressed backward; but this time he used the knife with method. The great snout was pressing his breast; the hot, fetid breath was in his nostrils; and at his shoulder the hungry eyes were glaring into his own. He struck for the left eye of the brute and struck true. The five-inch blade went in to the handle, piercing the brain, and the animal, with a convulsive spring which carried him half-way to his feet by the wounded arm, reared up, with paws outstretched, to full eight feet of length, then sagged down, and with a few spasmodic kicks, lay still. Rowland had done what no Innuit hunter will attempt —– he had fought and killed the Tiger-of-tbe-North with a knife.

It had all happened in a minute, but in that minute he was crippled for life; for in the quiet of a hospital, the best of surgical skill could hardly avail to reset the fractured particles of bone in the limp arm, and bring to place the crushed ribs. And he was adrift on a floating island of ice, with the temperature near the freezing point, and without even the rude appliances of the savage.

He painfully made his way to the little pile of red and white, and lifted it with his uninjured arm, though the stooping caused him excruciating torture. The child was bleeding from four deep, cruel scratches, extending diagonally from the right shoulder down the back; but he found upon examination that the soft, yielding bones were unbroken, and that her unconsciousness came from the rough contact of the little forehead with the ice; for a large lump had raised.

Futility: Or, The Wreck of the Titan

Of pure necessity, his first efforts must be made in his own behalf; so wrapping the baby in his coat he placed it in his shelter, and cut and made from the canvas a sling for his dangling arm. Then, with knife, fingers, and teeth, he partly skinned the bear —– often compelled to pause to save himself from fainting with pain —– and cut from the warm but not very thick layer of fat a broad slab, which, after bathing the wounds at a near–by pool, he bound firmly to the little one's back, using the torn night–gown for a bandage.

He cut the flannel lining from his coat, and from that of the sleeves made nether garments for the little limbs, doubling the surplus length over the ankles and tying in place with rope–yarns from a boatlacing. The body lining he wrapped around her waist, enclosing the arms, and around the whole he passed turn upon turn of canvas in strips, marling the mummy–like bundle with yarns, much as a sailor secures chafing–gear to the doubled parts of a hawser —— a process when complete, that would have aroused the indignation of any mother who saw it. But he was only a man, and suffering mental and physical anguish.

By the time he had finished, the child had recovered consciousness, and was protesting its misery in a feeble, wailing cry. But he dared not stop —— to become stiffened with cold and pain. There was plenty of fresh water from melting ice, scattered in pools. The bear would furnish food; but they needed fire, to cook this food, keep them warm, and the dangerous inflammation from their hurts, and to raise a smoke to be seen by passing craft.

He recklessly drank from the bottle, needing the stimulant, and reasoning, perhaps rightly, that no ordinary drug could affect him in his present condition; then he examined the wreckage —— most of it good kindling wood. Partly above, partly below the pile, was a steel lifeboat, decked over air–tight ends, now doubled to more than a right angle and resting on its side. With canvas hung over one half, and a small fire in the other, it promised, by its conducting property, a warmer and better shelter than the bridge. A sailor without matches is an anomaly. He whittled shavings, kindled the fire, hung the canvas and brought the child, who begged piteously for a drink of water.

He found a tin can —— possibly left in a leaky boat before its final boist to the davits —— and gave her a drink, to which he had added a few drops of the whisky. Then he thought of breakfast. Cutting a steak from the hindquarters of the bear, he toasted it on the end of a splinter and found it sweet and satisfying; but when he attempted to feed the child, he

26

understood the necessity of freeing its arms —– which he did, sacrificing his left shirtsleeve to cover them. The change and the food stopped its crying for a while, and Rowland lay down with it in the warm boat. Before the day had passed the whisky was gone and he was delirious with fever, while the child was but little better.

Chapter Nine

WITH lucid intervals, during which he replenished or rebuilt the fire, cooked the bear–meat, and fed and dressed the wounds of the child, this delirium lasted three days. His suffering was intense. His arm, the seat of throbbing pain, had swollen to twice the natural size, while his side prevented him taking a full breath, voluntarily. He had paid no attention to his own hurts, and it was either the vigor of a constitution that years of dissipation had not impaired, or some anti–febrile property of bear–meat, or the absence of the exciting whisky that won the battle. He rekindled the fire with his last match on the evening of the third day and looked around the darkening horizon, sane, but feeble in body and mind.

If a sail had appeared in the interim, he had not seen it; nor was there one in sight now. Too weak to climb the slope, he returned to the boat, where the child, exhausted from fruitless crying, was now sleeping. His unskillful and rather heroic manner of wrapping it up to protect it from cold had, no doubt, contributed largely to the closing of its wounds by forcibly keeping it still, though it must have added to its present sufferings. He looked for a moment on the wan, tear–stained little face, with its fringe of tangled curls peeping above the wrappings of canvas, and stooping painfully down, kissed it softly; but the kiss awakened it and it cried for its mother. He could not soothe it, nor could he try; and with a formless, wordless curse against destiny welling up from his heart, he left it and sat down on the wreckage at some distance away.

"We'll very likely get well," he mused, gloomily, unless I let the fire go out. What then? We can't last longer than the berg, and not much longer than the bear. We must be out of the tracks —– we were about nine hundred miles out when we struck; and the current sticks to the fog–belt here —– about westsou'west —– but that's the surface water. These deep fellows have currents of their own. There's no fog; we must be to the southward of the belt —– between the Lanes. They'll run their boats in the other Lane after this, I think —– the money–grabbing wretches. Curse them —– if they've drowned her. Curse them, with their water–tight compartments, and their logging of the lookouts. Twenty–four boats for three thousand people —– lashed down with tarred gripe–lashings —– thirty men to clear them away, and not an axe on the boat–deck or a sheath–knife on a man. Could she have got away? If they got that boat down, they might have taken her in from the steps; and the mate knew I had her child —– he would tell her. Her name must be Myra, too; it was her voice I heard in that dream. That was hasheesh. What did they drug me for? But the whisky was all right. It's all done with now, unless I get ashore —– but will I?"

The moon rose above the castellated structure to the left, flooding the icy beach with ashen–gray light, sparkling in a thousand points from the cascades, streams, and rippling pools, throwing into blackest shadow the gullies and hollows, and bringing to his mind, in spite of the weird beauty of the scene, a crushing sense of loneliness —– of littleness —– as though the vast pile of inorganic desolation which held him was of far greater importance than himself, and all the hopes, plans, and fears of his lifetime. The child bad cried itself to sleep again, and he paced up and down the ice.

"Up there," he said, moodily, looking into the sky, where a few stars shone faintly in the flood from the moon; "Up there —– somewhere —– they don't know just where —– but somewhere up above, is the Christians' Heaven. Up there is their good God —– who has placed Myra's child here —– their good God whom they borrowed from the savage, bloodthirsty race that invented him. And down below us —– somewhere again —– is their hell and their bad god, whom they invented themselves. And they give us our choice Heaven or hell. It is not so —– not so. The great mystery is not solved —– the human heart is not helped in this way. No good, merciful God created this world or its conditions. Whatever may be the nature of the causes at work beyond our mental vision, one fact is indubitably proven —– that the qualities of mercy, goodness, justice, play no part in the governing scheme. And yet, they say the core of all religions on earth is the belief in this. Is it? Or is it the cowardly, human fear of the unknown —– that impels the savage mother to throw her babe to a crocodile —– that impels the civilized man to endow churches —– that has kept in existence from the beginning a class of soothsayers, medicine–men, priests, and clergymen, all living on the hopes and fears excited by themselves.

"And people pray —– millions of them —– and claim they are answered. Are they? Was ever supplication sent into that sky by troubled humanity answered, or even heard? Who

28

knows? They pray for rain and sunshine, and both come in time. They pray for health and success and both are but natural in the marching of events. This is not evidence. But they say that they know, by spiritual uplifting, that they are heard, and comforted, and answered at the moment. Is not this a physiological experiment? Would they not feel equally tranquil if they repeated the multiplication table, or boxed the compass?

"Millions have believed tbis —— that prayers are answered —— and these millions have prayed to different gods. Were they all wrong or all right? Would a tentative prayer be listened to? Admitting that the Bibles, and Korans, and Vedas, are misleading and unreliable, may there not be an unseen, unknown Being, who knows my heart —— who is watching me now? If so, this Being gave me my reason, which doubts Him, and on Him is the responsibility. And would this being, if he exists, overlook a defect for which I am not to blame, and listen to a prayer from me, based on the mere chance that I might be mistaken? Can an unbeliever, in the full strength of his reasoning powers, come to such trouble that he can no longer stand alone, but must cry for help to an imagined power? Can such time come to a sane man —— to me? "He looked at the dark line of vacant horizon. It was seven miles away; New York was nine hundred; the moon in the east over two hundred thousand, and the stars above, any number of billions. He was alone, with a sleeping child, a dead bear, and the Unknown. He walked softly to the boat and looked at the little one for a moment; then, raising his head, he whispered: "For you, Myra."

Sinking to his knees the atheist lifted his eyes to the heavens, and with his feeble voice and the fervor born of helplessness, prayed to the God that he denied. He begged for the life of the waif in his care —— for the safety of the mother, so needful to the little one —— and for courage and strength to do his part and bring them together. But beyond the appeal for help in the service of others, not one word or expressed thought of his prayer included himself as a beneficiary. So much for pride. As he rose to his feet, the flying–jib of a bark appeared around the corner of ice to the right of the beach, and a moment later the whole moon–lit fabric came into view, wafted along by the faint westerly air, not half a mile away.

He sprang to the fire, forgetting his pain, and throwing on wood, made a blaze. He hailed, in a frenzy of excitement: "Bark ahoy! Bark ahoy! Take us off," and a deep–toned answer came across the water.

"Wake up, Myra," he cried, as he lifted the child; "wake up. We're going away."

"We goin' to mamma?" she asked, with no symptoms of crying.

"Yes, we're going to mamma now —– that is," he added to himself; "if that clause in the prayer is considered."

Fifteen minutes later as he watched the approach of a white quarter–boat, he muttered: "That bark was there —– half a mile back in this wind —– before I thought of praying. Is that prayer answered? Is she safe?"

Chapter Ten

ON the first floor of the London Royal Exchange is a large apartment studded with desks, around and between which surges a hurrying, shouting crowd of brokers, clerks, and messengers. Fringing this apartment are doors and hallways leading to adjacent rooms and offices, and scattered through it are bulletin–boards, on which are daily written in duplicate the marine casualties of the world. At one end is a raised platform, sacred to the presence of an important functionary. In the technical language of the "City," the apartment is known as the "Room," and the functionary, as the "Caller," whose business it is to call out in a mighty sing–song voice the names of members wanted at the door, and the bare particulars of bulletin news prior to its being chalked out for reading.

It is the headquarters of Lloyds —— tbe immense association of underwriters, brokers, and shipping–men, which, beginning with the customers at Edward Lloyd's coffeehouse in the latter part of the seventeentb century, has, retaining his name for a title, developed into a corporation so well equipped, so splendidly organized and powerful, that kings and ministers of state appeal to it at times for foreign news.

Not a master or mate sails under the English flag but whose record, even to forecastle fights, is tabulated at Lloyds for the inspection of prospective employers. Not a ship is cast away on any inhabitable coast of the world, during underwriters' business hours, but what that mighty sing–song cry announces the event at Lloyds within thirty minutes.

One of the adjoining rooms is known as the Chartroom. Here can be found in perfect order and sequence, each on its roller, the newest charts of all nations, with a library of nautical literature describing to the last detail the harbors, lights, rocks, shoals, and sailing directions of every coast–line shown on the charts; the tracks of latest storms; the changes of ocean currents, and the whereabouts of derelicts and icebergs. A member at Lloyds acquires in time a theoretical knowledge of the sea seldom exceeded by the men who navigate it.

Another apartment —– the Captain's room —– is given over to joy and refreshment, and still another, the antithesis of the last, is the Intelligence office, where anxious ones inquire for and are told the latest news of this or that overdue ship.

On the day when the assembled throng of underwriters and brokers had been thrown into an uproarious panic the Crier's announcement that the great Titan was destroyed, and the papers of Europe and America were issuing extras giving the meager details of the arrival at New York of one boat–load of her people, this office had been crowded with weeping women and worrying men, who would ask, and remain to ask again, for more news. And when it came —– a later cablegram, —– giving the story of the wreck and the names of the captain, first officer, boatswain, seven sailors, and one lady passenger as those of the saved, a feeble old gentleman had raised his voice in a quavering scream, high above the sobbing of women, and said:

"My daughter–in–law is safe; but where is my son, —– where is my son, and my grandchild? "Then he had hurried away, but was back again the next day, and the next. And when, on the tenth day of waiting and watching, he learned of another boat–load of sailors and children arrived at Gibraltar, he shook his head, slowly, muttering: "George, George," and left the room. That night, after telegraphing the consul at Gibraltar of his coming, he crossed the channel.

In the first tumultuous riot of inquiry, when underwriters had climbed over desks and each other to hear again of the wreck of the Titan, one —– the noisest of all, a corpulent, hook–nosed man with flashing black eyes —– had broken away from the crowd and made his way to the Captain's room, where, after a draught of brandy, he had seated himself heavily, with a groan that came from his soul.

"Father Abraham," be muttered; "this will ruin me."

Others came in, some to drink, some to condole —– all, to talk.

Futility: Or, The Wreck of the Titan

"Hard hit, Meyer?" asked one.

"Ten thousand," he answered, gloomily.

"Serve you right," said another, unkindly; "have more baskets for your eggs. Knew you'd bring up."

Though Mr. Meyer's eyes sparkled at this, he said nothing, but drank himself stupid and was assisted home by one of his clerks. From this on, neglecting his business —– excepting to occasionally visit the bulletins —– he spent his time in the Captain's room drinking heavily, and bemoaning his luck. On the tenth day be read with watery eyes, posted on the bulletin below the news of the arrival at Gibraltar of the second boat–load of people, the following:

"Life–buoy of Royal Age, London, picked up among wreckage in Lat. 45–20, N. Lon. 54–31 W. Ship Arctic, Boston, Capt. Brandt."

"Oh, mine good God," he bowled, as he rushed toward the Captain's room.

"Poor devil —– poor damn fool of an Israelite," said one observer to another. "He covered the whole of the Royal Age, and the biggest chunk of the Titan. It'll take his wife's diamonds to settle."

Three weeks later, Mr. Meyer was aroused from a brooding lethargy, by a crowd of shouting underwriters, who rushed into the Captain's room, seized him by the shoulders, and hurried him out and up to a bulletin.

"Read it, Meyer —– read it. What d'you think of it?" With some difficulty he read aloud, while they watched his face:

"John Rowland, sailor of the Titan, with child passenger, name unknown, on board Peerless, Bath, at Christiansand, Norway. Both dangerously ill. Rowland speaks of ship cut in half night before loss of Titan."

"What do you make of it, Meyer —– Royal Age, isn't it? " asked one.

"Yes," vociferated another, "I've figured back. Only ship not reported lately. Overdue two months. Was spoken same day fifty miles east of that iceberg."

"Sure thing," said others. "Nothing said about it in the captain's statement —– looks queer."

"Vell, vwhat of it," said Mr. Meyer, painfully and stupidly: "dere is a collision clause in der Titan's policy; I merely bay the money to der steamship company instead of to der Royal Age beeple."

"But why did the captain conceal it?" they shouted at him. "What's his object —– assured against collision suits."

"Der looks of it, berhaps —– looks pad."

"Nonsense, Meyer, what's the matter with you? Which one of the lost tribes did you spring from —– you're like none of your race —– drinking yourself stupid like a good Christian. I've got a thousand on the , and if I'm to pay it I want to know why. You've got the heaviest risk and the brain to fight for it —– you've got to do it. Go home, straighten up, and attend to this. We'll watch Rowland till you take hold. We're all caught."

They put him into a cab, took him to a Turkish bath, and then home.

The next morning he was at his desk, clear–eyed and clear–headed, and for a few weeks was a busy, scheming man of business.

Chapter Eleven

ON a certain morning, about two months after the announcement of the loss of the Titan, Mr. Meyer sat at his desk in the Rooms, busily writing, when the old gentleman who had bewailed the death of his son in the Intelligence office tottered in and took a chair beside him.

"Good morning, Mr. Selfridge," he said, scarcely looking up; "I suppose you have come to see der insurance paid over. Der sixty days are up."

"Yes, yes, Mr. Meyer," said the old gentleman, wearily; "of course, as merely a stockholder, I can take no active part; but I am a member here, and naturally a little anxious. All I had in the world —— even to my son and grandchild —— was in the Titan."

"It is very sad, Mr. Selfridge; you have my deepest sympathy. I pelieve you are der largest holder of Titan stock —– about one hundred thousand, is it not?"

"About that."

"I am der heaviest insurer; so Mr. Selfridge, this battle will be largely petween you and myself."

"Battle —— is there to be any difficulty?" asked Mr. Selfridge, anxiously.

"Berhaps —– I do not know. Der underwriters and outside companies have blaced matters in my hands and will not bay until I take der initiative. We must hear from one John Rowland, who, with a little child, was rescued from der berg and taken to Christiansand. He has been too sick to leave der ship which found him and is coming up der Thames in her this morning. I have a carriage at der dock and expect him at my office by noon. Dere is where we will dransact this little pizness —— not here."

"A child —– saved," queried the old gentleman; dear me, it may be little Myra. She was not at Gibraltar with the others. I would not care —— I would not care much about the money, if she was safe. But my son —– my only son —— is gone; and, Mr. Meyer, I am a ruined man if this insurance is not paid."

"And I am a ruined man if it is," said Mr. Meyer, rising. "Will you come around to der office, Mr. Selfridge? I expect der attorney and Captain Bryce are dere now." Mr. Selfridge arose and accompanied him to the street.

A rather meagerly–furnished private office in Threadneedle Street, partitioned off from a larger one bearing Mr. Meyer's name in the window, received the two men, one of whom, in the interests of good business, was soon to be impoverished. They had not waited a minute before Captain Bryce and Mr. Austen were announced and ushered in. Sleek, well–fed, and gentlemanly in manner, perfect types of the British naval officer, they bowed politely to Mr. Selfridge when Mr. Meyer introduced them as the captain and first officer of the Titan, and seated themselves. A few moments later brought a shrewd looking person whom Mr. Meyer addressed as the attorney for the steamship company, but did not introduce; for such are the amenities of the English system of caste.

"Now then, gentlemen," said Mr. Meyer, "I pelieve we can broceed to pizness up to a certain point —– berbaps further. Mr. Thompson, you have the affidavit of Captain Bryce?"

"I have," said the attorney, producing a document which Mr. Meyer glanced at and handed back.

"And in this statement, captain, he said, "you have sworn that der voyage was uneventful up to der moment of der wreck —– that is," be added, with an oily smile, as be noticed the paling of the captain's face "that nothing occurred to make der Titan less seaworthy or manageable?"

"That is what I swore to," said the captain, with a little sigh.

"You are part owner, are you not, Captain Bryce?"

"I own five shares of the company's stock."

"I have examined der charter and der company lists," said Mr. Meyer; "each boat of der company is, so far as assessments and dividends are concerned, a separate company. I find you are listed as owning two sixty—seconds of der Titan stock. This makes you, under der law, part owner of der Titan, and responsible as such."

"What do you mean, sir, by that word responsible?" said Captain Bryce, quicky.

For answer, Mr. Meyer elevated his black eyebrows, assumed an attitude of listening, looked at his watch and went to the door, which, as he opened, admitted the sound of carriage wheels.

"In here," be called to his clerks, then faced the captain.

Futility: Or, The Wreck of the Titan

"What do I mean, Captain Bryce?" he thundered. "I mean that you have concealed in your sworn statement all reference to der fact that you collided with and sunk the ship Royal Age on der night before the wreck of your own ship."

"Who says so —– how do you know it?" blustered the captain. "You have only that bulletin statement of the man Rowland —– an irresponsible drunkard."

"The man was lifted aboard drunk at New York," broke in the first officer, "and remained in a condition of delirium tremens up to the shipwreck. We did not meet the Royal Age and are in no way responsible for her loss."

"Yes," added Captain Bryce, "and a man in that condition is liable to see anything. We listened to his ravings on the night of the wreck. He was on lookout —– on the bridge. Mr. Austen, the boats'n, and myself were close to him."

Before Mr. Meyer's oily smile had indicated to the flustered captain that he had said too much, the door opened and admitted Rowland, pale, and weak, with empty left sleeve, leaning on the arm of a bronze–bearded and manly–looking giant who carried little Myra on the other shoulder, and who said, in the breezy tone of the quarter–deck:

"Well, I've brought him, half dead; but why couldn't you give me time to dock my ship? A mate can't do everything."

"And this is Captain Barry, of der Peerless," said Mr. Meyer, taking his hand. "It is all right, my friend; you will not lose. And this is Mr. Rowland —– and this is der little child. Sit down, my friend. I congratulate you on your escape."

"Thank you," said Rowland, weakly, as he seated himself; "they cut my arm off at Christiansand, and I still live. That is my escape."

Captain Bryce and Mr. Austen, pale and motionless, stared hard at this man, in whose emaciated face, refined by suffering to the almost spiritual softness of age, they hardly recognized the features of the troublesome sailor of the Titan. His clothing, though clean, was ragged and patched.

Mr. Selfridge had arisen and was also staring, not at Rowland, but at the child, who, seated in the lap of the big Captain Barry, was looking around with wondering eyes. Her costume was unique. A dress of bagging–stuff, put together —— as were her canvas shoes and hat —– with sail–twine in sail–makers' stitches, three to the inch, covered skirts and underclothing made from old flannel shirts. It represented many an hour's work of the watch–below, lovingly bestowed by the crew of the Peerless; for the crippled Rowland could not sew. Mr. Selfridge approached, scanned the pretty features closely, and asked:

"What is her name?"

"Her first name is Myra," answered Rowland. "She remembers that; but I have not learned her last name, though I knew her mother years ago —— before her marriage."

"Myra, Myra," repeated the old gentleman; "do you know me? Don't you know me? " He trembled visibly as he stooped and kissed her. The little forehead puckered and wrinkled as the child struggled with memory; then it cleared and the whole face sweetened to a smile.

"Gwampa," she said.

"Oh, God, I thank thee," murmured Mr. Selfridge, taking her in his arms. "I have lost my son, but I have found his child —— my granddaughter."

"But, sir," asked Rowland, eagerly; "you —— this child's grandfather? Your son is lost, you say? Was he on board the Titan? And the mother —— was she saved, or is she, too ——" he stopped unable to continue.

"The mother is safe —— in New York; but the father, my son, has not yet been heard from," said the old man, mournfully.

Rowland's head sank and he hid his face for a moment in his arm, on the table at which he sat. It had been a face as old, and worn, and weary as that of the white–haired man confronting him. On it, when it raised —— flushed, bright–eyed and smiling —— was the glory of youth.

"I trust, sir," he said, "that you will telegraph her. I am penniless at present, and, besides, do not know her name."

"Selfridge —– which, of course, is my own name. Mrs. Colonel, or Mrs. George Selfridge. Our New York address is well known. But I shall cable her at once; and, believe me, sir, although I can understand that our debt to you cannot be named in terms of money, you need not be penniless long. You are evidently a capable man, and I have wealth and influence."

Rowland merely bowed, slightly, but Mr. Meyer muttered to himself: "Vealth and influence. Berhaps not. Now, gentlemen," he added, in a louder tone, "to pizness. Mr. Rowland, will you tell us about der running down of der Royal Age?"

"Was it the Royal Age?" asked Rowland. "I sailed in her one voyage. Yes, certainly."

Mr. Selfridge, more interested in Myra than in the coming account, carried her over to a chair in the corner and sat down, where he fondled and talked to her after the manner of grandfathers the world over, and Rowland, first looking steadily into the faces of the two men he had come to expose, and whose presence he had thus far ignored, told, while they held their teeth tight together and often buried their finger–nails in their palms, the terrible story of the cutting in half of the ship on the first night out from New York, finishing with the attempted bribery and his refusal.

"Vell, gentlemen, vwhat do you think of that? asked Mr. Meyer, looking around.

"A lie, from beginning to end," stormed Captain Bryce.

Rowland rose to his feet, but was pressed back by the big man who had accompanied him —– who then faced Captain Bryce and said, quietly:

"I saw a polar bear that this man killed in open fight. I saw his arm afterward, and while nursing him away from death I heard no whines or complaints. He can fight his own battles when well, and when sick I'll do it for him. If you insult him again in my presence I'll knock your teeth down your throat."

Chapter Twelve

THERE was a moment's silence while the two captains eyed one another, broken by the attorney, who said:

"Whether this story is true or false, it certainly has no bearing on the validity of the policy. If this happened, it was after the policy attached and before the wreck of the Titan."

"But der concealment —– der concealment," shouted Mr. Meyer, excitedly.

"Has no bearing, either. If he concealed anything it was done after the wreck, and after your liability was confirmed. It was not even barratry. You must pay this insurance."

"I will not bay it. I will not. I will fight you in der courts." Mr. Meyer stamped up and down the floor in his excitement, then stopped with a triumphant smile, and shook his finger into the face of the attorney.

"And even if der concealment will not vitiate der policy, der fact that he had a drunken man on lookout when der Titan struck der iceberg will be enough. Go ahead and sue. I will not pay. He was part owner."

"You have no witnesses to that admission," said the attorney. Mr. Meyer looked around the group and the smile left his face.

"Captain Bryce was mistaken," said Mr. Austen. This man was drunk at New York, like others of the crew. But he was sober and competent when on lookout. I discussed theories of navigation with him during his trick on the bridge that night and be spoke intelligently."

"But you yourself said, not ten minutes ago, that this man was in a state of delirium tremens up to der collision," said Mr. Meyer.

"What I said and what I will admit under oath are two different things," said the officer, desperately. "I may have said anything under the excitement of the moment —– when we were accused of such an infamous crime. I say now, that John Rowland, whatever may have been his condition on the preceding night, was a sober and competent lookout at the time of the wreck of the Titan."

"Thank you," said Rowland, dryly, to the first officer; then, looking into the appealing face of Mr. Meyer, he said:

"I do not think it will be necessary to brand me before the world as an inebriate in order to punish the company and these men. Barratry, as I understand it, is the unlawful act of a captain or crew at sea, causing damage or loss; and it only applies when the parties are purely employees. Did I understand rightly —– that Captain Bryce was part owner of the Titan?"

"Yes," said Mr. Meyer, "he owns stock; and we insure against barratry; but this man, as part owner, could not fall back on it."

"And an unlawful act," went on Rowland, "perpetrated by a captain who is part owner, which might cause shipwreck, and, during the perpetration of which shipwreck really occurs, will be sufficient to void the policy."

"Certainly," said Mr. Meyer, eagerly. "You were drunk on der lookout —– you were raving drunk, as he said himself. You will swear to this, will you not, my friend? It is bad faith with der underwriters. It annuls der insurance. You admit this, Mr. Thompson, do you not?"

"That is law," said the attorney, coldly.

"Was Mr. Austen a part owner, also?" asked Rowland, ignoring Mr. Meyer's view of the case.

"One share, is it not, Mr. Austen?" asked Mr. Meyer, while he rubbed his hands and smiled. Mr. Austen made no sign of denial and Rowland continued:

"Then, for drugging a sailor into a stupor, and having him on lookout out of his turn while in that condition, and at the moment when the Titan struck the iceberg, Captain Bryce and Mr. Austen have, as part owners, committed an act which nullifies the insurance on that ship."

"You infernal, lying scoundrel! "roared Captain Bryce. He strode toward Rowland with threatening face. Half—way, he was stopped by the impact of a huge brown fist which sent him reeling and staggering across the room toward Mr. Selfridge and the child, over whom he floundered to the floor —— a disheveled heap, —— while the big Captain Barry examined teeth—marks on his knuckles, and every one else sprang to their feet.

"I told you to look out," said Captain Barry. Treat my friend respectfully." He glared steadily at the first officer, as though inviting him to duplicate the offense; but that gentleman backed away from him and assisted the dazed Captain Bryce to a chair,where be felt of his loosened teeth, spat blood upon Mr. Meyer's floor, and gradually awakened to a realization of the fact that he had been knocked down —— and by an American.

Little Myra, unhurt but badly frightened, began to cry and call for Rowland in her own way, to the wonder, and somewhat to the scandal of the gentle old man who was endeavoring to soothe her.

"Dammy," she cried, as she struggled to go to him; "Iwant Dammy —— Dammy —— Da—a—may."

"Oh, what a pad little girl," said the jocular Mr. Meyer, looking down on her. "Where did you learn such language?"

"It is my nickname," said Rowland, smiling in spite of himself. "She has coined the word," he explained to the agitated Mr. Selfridge, who had not yet comprehended what had happened; "and I have not yet been able to persuade her to drop it —— and I could not be harsh with her. Let me take her, sir." He seated himself, with the child, who nestled up to him contentedly and soon was tranquil.

"Now, my friend," said Mr. Meyer, "you must tell us about this drugging." Then while Captain Bryce, under the memory of the blow he had received, nursed himself into an insane fury; and Mr. Austen, with his hand resting lightly on the captain's shoulder ready to restrain him, listened to the story; and the attorney drew up a chair and took notes of the story; and Mr. Selfridge drew his chair close to Myra and paid no attention to the story at all, Rowland recited the events prior to and succeeding the shipwreck. Beginning

41

with the finding of the whisky in his pocket, he told of his being called to the starboard bridge lookout in place of the rightful incumbent; of the sudden and strange interest Mr. Austen displayed as to his knowledge of navigation; of the pain in his stomach, the frightful shapes he had seen on the deck beneath and the sensations of his dream —— leaving out only the part which bore on the woman be loved; he told of the sleep–walking child which awakened him, of the crash of ice and instant wreck, and the fixed condition of his eyes which prevented their focusing only at a certain distance, finishing his story —– to explain his empty sleeve —– with a graphic account of the fight with the bear.

"And I have studied it all out," be said, in conclusion. "I was drugged —— I believe, with hasheesh, which makes a man see strange things —— and brought up on the bridge lookout where I could be watched and my ravings listened to and recorded, for the sole purpose of discrediting my threatened testimony in regard to the collision of the night before. But I was only half–drugged, as I spilled part of my tea at supper. In that tea, I am positive, was the hasheesh."

"You know all about it, don't you," snarled Captain Bryce, from his chair, "'twas not hasheesh; 'twas an infusion of Indian hemp; you don't know —–" Mr. Austen's hand closed over his mouth and he subsided.

"Self–convicted," said Rowland, with a quiet laugh. "Hasheesh is made from Indian hemp."

"You hear this, gentlemen," exclaimed Mr. Meyer, springing to his feet and facing everybody in turn. He pounced on Captain Barry. "You hear this confession, captain; you hear him say Indian hemp? I have a witness now, Mr. Thompson. Go right on with your suit. You hear him, Captain Barry. You are disinterested. You are a witness. You hear?"

"Yes, I heard it —– the murdering scoundrel," said the captain.

Mr. Meyer danced up and down in his joy, while the attorney, pocketing his notes, remarked to the discomfited Captain Bryce: "You are the poorest fool I know," and left the office.

42

Then Mr. Meyer calmed himself, and facing the two steamship officers, said, slowly and impressively, while be poked his forefinger almost into their faces:

"England is a fine country, my friends —– a fine country to leave pebind sometimes. Dere is Canada, and der United States, and Australia, and South Africa —– all fine countries, too —– fine countries to go to with new names. My friends, you will be bulletened and listed at Lloyds in less than half an hour, and you will never again sail under der English flag as officers. And, my friends, let me say, that in half an hour after you are bulletened, all Scotland Yard will be looking for you. But my door is not locked."

Silently they arose, pale, shamefaced, and crushed, and went out the door, through the outer office, and into the street.

Chapter Thirteen

MR SELFRIDGE had begun to take an interest in the proceedings. As the two men passed out he arose and asked:

"Have you reached a settlement, Mr. Meyer? Will the insurance be paid?"

"No," roared the underwriter, in the ear of the puzzled old gentleman; while he slapped him vigorously on the back; "it will not be paid. You or I must have been ruined, Mr. Selfridge, and it has settled on you. I do not pay der Titan's insurance —— nor will der other insurers. On der contrary, as der collision clause in der policy is void with der rest, your company must reimburse me for der insurance which I must pay to der Royal Age owners —— that is, unless our good friend here, Mr. Rowland, who was on der lookout at der time, will swear that her lights were out."

"Not at all," said Rowland. "Her lights were burning —— look to the old gentleman," be exclaimed. "Look out for him. Catch him! "

Mr. Selfridge was stumbling toward a chair. He grasped it, loosened his hold, and before anyone could reach him, fell to the floor, where be lay, with ashen lips and rolling eyes gasping convulsively.

Heart failure," said Rowland, as he knelt by his side. "Send for a doctor."

"Send for a doctor," repeated Mr. Meyer through the door to his clerks; "and send for a carriage, quick. I don't want him to die in der office."

Captain Barry lifted the helpless figure to a couch, and they watched, while the convulsions grew easier, the breath sborter, and the lips from ashen gray to blue. Before a doctor or carriage had come, he had passed away.

"Sudden emotion of some kind," said the doctor when be did arrive. "Violent emotion, too. Hear bad news?"

"Bad and good," answered the underwriter. Good, in learning that this dear little girl was his granddaughter —– bad, in learning that he was a ruined man. He was der heaviest stockholder in der Titan. One hundred thousand pounds, be owned, of der stock, all of which this poor, dear little child will not get." Mr. Meyer looked sorrowful, as be patted Myra on the head.

Captain Barry beckoned to Rowland, who, slightly flushed, was standing by the still figure on the couch and watching the face of Mr. Meyer, on which annoyance, jubilation, and simulated shock could be seen in turn.

"Wait," he said, as he turned to watch the doctor leave the room. "Is this so, Mr. Meyer," he added to the underwriter, "that Mr. Selfridge owned Titan stock, and would have been ruined, had he lived, by the loss of the insurance money?"

"Yes, he would have been a poor man. He had invested his last farthing —– one hundred thousand pounds. And if he had left any more it would be assessed to make good his share of what der company must bay for der Royal Age, which I also insured."

"Was there a collision clause in the Titan',s policy?"

"Dere was."

"And you took the risk, knowing that she was to run the Northern Lane at full speed through fog and snow?"

I did —– so did others.

Then, Mr. Meyer, it remains for me to tell you that the insurance on the Titan will be paid, as well as any liabilities included in and specified by the collision clause in the policy. In short, I, the one man who can prevent it, refuse to testify."

"Vwbat−a−t?"

Mr. Meyer grasped the back of a chair and, leaning over it, stared at Rowland.

"You will not testify? Vwbat you mean?"

"What I said; and I do not feel called upon to give you my reasons, Mr. Meyer."

"My good friend," said the underwriter, advancing with outstretched hands to Rowland, who backed away, and taking Myra by the hand, moved toward the door. Mr. Meyer sprang ahead, locked it and removed the key, and faced them.

"Oh, mine goot Gott," he shouted, relapsing in his excitement into the more pronounced dialect of his race; "vwbat I do to you, hey? Vwhy you go pack on me, hey? Haf I not bay der doctor's bill? Haf I not bay for der carriage? Haf I not treat you like one shentleman? Haf I not, hey? I sit you down in mine office and call you Mr. Rowland. Haf I not been one shentleman?"

"Open that door," said Rowland, quietly.

"Yes, open it," repeated Captain Barry, his puzzled face clearing at the prospect of action on his part. "Open it or I'll kick it down."

"But you, mine friend —– heard der admission of der captain —– of der drugging. One goot witness will do: two is petter. But you will swear, mine friend, you will not ruin me."

"I stand by Rowland," said the captain, grimly. "I don't remember what was said, anyhow; got a blamed bad memory. Get away from that door."

Futility: Or, The Wreck of the Titan

Grievous lamentation —— weepings and wailings, and the most genuine gnashing of teeth —— interspersed with the feebler cries of the frightened Myra and punctuated by terse commands in regard to the door, filled that private office, to the wonder of the clerks without, and ended, at last, with the crashing of the door from its binges.

Captain Barry, Rowland, and Myra, followed by a parting, heart–borne malediction from the agitated underwriter, left the office and reached the street. The carriage that had brought them was still waiting.

"Settle inside," called the captain to the driver. We'll take another, Rowland."

Around the first corner they found a cab, which they entered, Captain Barry giving the driver the directions —— "Bark Peerless, East India Dock."

"I think I understand the game, Rowland," he said, as they started; "you don't want to break this child."

"That's it," answered Rowland, weakly, as he leaned back on the cushion, faint from the excitement of the last few moments. "And as for the right or wrong of the position I am in —— why, we must go farther back for it than the question of lookouts. The cause of the wreck was full speed in a fog. All hands on lookout could not have seen that berg. The underwriters knew the speed and took the risk. Let them pay."

"Right —— and I'm with you on it. But you must get out of the country. I don't know the law on the matter, but they may compel you to testify. You can't ship 'fore the mast again —— that's settled. But you can have a berth mate with me as long as I sail a sbip —— if you'll take it; and you're to make my cabin your home as long as you like; remember that. Still, I know you want to get across with the kid, and if you stay around until I sail it may be months before you get to New York, with the chance of losing her by getting foul of English law. But just leave it to me. There are powerful interests at stake in regard to this matter."

What Captain Barry had in mind, Rowland was too weak to inquire. On their arrival at the bark be was assisted by his friend to a couch in the cabin, where be spent the rest of the day, unable to leave it. Meanwhile, Captain Barry had gone ashore again.

Futility: Or, The Wreck of the Titan

Returning toward evening, he said to the man on the couch: "I've got your pay, Rowland, and signed a receipt for it to that attorney. He paid it out of his own pocket. You could have worked that company for fifty thousand, or more; but I knew you wouldn't touch their money, and so, only struck him for your wages. You're entitled to a month's pay. Here it is —— American money–about seventeen." He gave Rowland a roll of bills.

"Now here's something else, Rowland," he continued, producing an envelope. "In consideration of the fact that you lost all your clothes and later, your arm, through the carelessness of the company's officers, Mr. Thompson offers you this." Rowland opened the envelope. In it were two first cabin tickets from Liverpool to New York. Flushing hotly, he said, bitterly:

"It seems that I'm not to escape it, after all."

"Take 'em, old man, take 'em; in fact, I took 'em for you, and you and the kid are booked. And I made Thompson agree to settle your doctor's bill and expenses with that Sheeny. 'Tisn't bribery. I'd heel you myself for the run over, but, hang it, you'll take nothing from me. You've got to get the young un over. You're the only one to do it. The old gentleman was an American, alone here —— hadn't even a lawyer, that I could find. The boat sails in the morning and the night train leaves in two hours. Think of that mother, Rowland. Why, man, I'd travel round the world to stand in your shoes when you hand Myra over. I've got a child of my own." The captain's eyes were winking hard and fast, and Rowland's were shining.

"Yes, I'll take the passage," he said, with a smile. I accept the bribe."

"That's right. You'll be strong and healthy when you land, and when that mother's through thanking you, and you have to think of yourself, remember —— I want a mate and will be here a month before sailing. Write to me, care o' Lloyds, if you want the berth, and I'll send you advance money to get back with."

"Thank you, captain," said Rowland, as he took the other's hand and then glanced at his empty sleeve; "but my going to sea is ended. Even a mate needs two hands."

"Well, suit yourself, Rowland; I'll take you mate without any hands at all while you had your brains. It's done me good to meet a man like you; and —— say, old man, you won't

47

take it wrong from me, will you? It's none o' my business, but you're too all–fired good a man to drink. You haven't had a nip for two months. Are you going to begin?"

"Never again," said Rowland, rising. "I've a future now, as well as a past."

Chapter Fourteen

IT was near noon of the next day that Rowland, seated in a steamer–chair with Myra and looking out on a sail–spangled stretch of blue from the saloon–deck of a west–bound liner, remembered that he had made no provisions to have Mrs. Selfridge notified by cable of the safety of her child; and unless Mr. Meyer or his associates gave the story to the press it would not be known.

"Well," he mused, "joy will not kill, and I shall witness it in its fullness if I take her by surprise. But the chances are that it will get into the papers before I reach her. It is too good for Mr. Meyer to keep."

But the story was not given out immediately. Mr. Meyer called a conference of the underwriters concerned with him in the insurance of the Titan at which it was decided to remain silent concerning the card they hoped to play, and to spend a little time and money in hunting for other witnesses among the Titan's crew, and in interviewing Captain Barry, to the end of improving his memory. A few stormy meetings with this huge obstructionist convinced them of the futility of further effort in his direction, and, after finding at the end of a week that every surviving member of the Titan's port watch, as well as a few of the other, had been induced to sign for Cape voyages, or had otherwise disappeared, they decided to give the story told by Rowland to the press in the hope that publicity would avail to bring to light corroboratory evidence.

And this story, improved upon in the repeating by Mr. Meyer to reporters, and embellished still further by the reporters as they wrote it up, particularly in the part pertaining to the polar bear, —— blazoned out in the great dailies of England and the Continent, and was cabled to New York, with the name of the steamer in which John Rowland had sailed (for his movements had been traced in the search for evidence), where it arrived, too late for publication, the morning of the day on which, with Myra on his shoulder, he stepped down the gangplank at a North River dock. As a consequence, he was surrounded on the dock by enthusiastic reporters, who spoke of the story and asked for details. He refused to talk, escaped them, and gaining the side streets, soon found himself in crowded Broadway, where be entered the office of the steamship company in whose employ he had been wrecked, and secured from the Titan's passenger–list the address of Mrs. Selfridge —— the only woman saved. Then he took a car up Broadway and alighted abreast of a large department store.

"We're going to see mamma, soon, Myra," he whispered in the pink ear; "and you must go dressed up. It don't matter about me; but you're a Fifth Avenue baby —— a little aristocrat. These old clothes won't do, now." But she had forgotten the word "mamma," and was more interested in the exciting noise and life of the street than in the clothing she wore. In the store, Rowland asked for, and was directed to the children's department, where a young woman waited on him.

"This child has been shipwrecked," he said. "I have sixteen dollars and a half to spend on it. Give it a bath, dress its hair, and use up the money on a dress, shoes, and stockings, underclothing, and a hat." The young woman stooped and kissed the little girl from sheer sympathy, but protested that not much could be done.

"Do your best," said Rowland; "it is all I have. I will wait here."

An hour later, penniless again, he emerged from the store with Myra, bravely dressed in her new finery, and was stopped at the corner by a policeman who had seen him come out, and who marveled, doubtless, at such juxtaposition of rags and ribbons.

"Whose kid ye got?" he demanded.

"I believe it is the daughter of Mrs. Colonel Selfridge," answered Rowland, haughtily —— too haughtily, by far.

"Ye believe —— but ye don't know. Come back into the shtore, me tourist, and we'll see who ye shtole it from."

"Very well, officer; I can prove possession." They started back, the officer with his hand on Rowland's collar, and were met at the door by a party of three or four people coming out. One of this party, a young woman in black, uttered a piercing shriek and sprang toward them.

"Myra!" she screamed. "Give me my baby —– give her to me."

She snatched the child from Rowland's shoulder, hugged it, kissed it, cried, and screamed over it; then, oblivious to the crowd that collected, incontinently fainted in the arms of an indignant old gentleman.

"You scoundrel!" he exclaimed, as he flourished his cane over Rowland's head with his free arm. "We've caught you. Officer, take that man to the station–house. I will follow and make a charge in the name of my daughter."

"Then he shtole the kid, did he?" asked the policeman.

"Most certainly," answered the old gentleman, as, with the assistance of the others, he supported the unconscious young mother to a carriage. They all entered, little Myra screaming for Rowland from the arms of a female member of the party, and were driven off.

"C'm an wi' me," uttered the officer, rapping his prisoner on the head with his club and jerking him off his feet.

Then, while an approving crowd applauded, the man who had fought and conquered a hungry polar bear was dragged through the streets like a sick animal by a New York policeman. For such is the stultifying effect of a civilized environment.

Chapter Fifteen

IN New York City there are homes permeated by a moral atmosphere so pure, so elevated, so sensitive to the vibrations of human woe and misdoing, that their occupants are removed completely from all consideration of any but the spiritual welfare of poor humanity. In these homes the news–gathering, sensation–mongering daily paper does not enter.

In the same city are dignified magistrates —– memhers of clubs and societies —– who spend late hours, and often fail to arise in the morning in time to read the papers before the opening of court.

Also in New York are city editors, bilious of stomach, testy of speech, and inconsiderate of reporters' feelings and professional pride. Such editors, when a reporter has failed, through no fault of his own, in successfully interviewing a celebrity, will sometimes send him news–gathering in the police courts, where printable news is scarce.

On the morning following the arrest of John Rowland, three reporters, sent by three such editors, attended a hall of justice presided over by one of the late–rising magistrates mentioned above. In the anteroom of this court, ragged, disfigured by his clubbing, and disheveled by his night in a cell, stood Rowland, with other unfortunates more or less guilty of offense against society. When his name was called, he was hustled through a door, along a line of policemen —– each of whom added to his own usefulness by giving him a shove and into the dock, where the stern–faced and tired–looking magistrate glared at him. Seated in a corner of the court–room were the old gentleman of the day before, the young mother with little Myra in her lap, and a number of other ladies —– all excited in demeanor; and all but the young mother directing venomous glances at Rowland. Mrs. Selfridge, pale and hollow–eyed, but happy–faced, withal, allowed no wandering glance to rest on him.

The officer who had arrested Rowland was sworn, and testified that he had stopped the prisoner on Broadway while making off with the child, whose rich clothing had attracted his attention. Disdainful sniffs were heard in the corner with muttered remarks: "Rich indeed —– the idea —– the flimsiest prints." Mr. Gaunt, the prosecuting witness, was called to testify.

"This man, your Honor," he began, excitedly, "was once a gentleman and a frequent guest at my house. He asked for the hand of my daughter, and as his request was not granted, threatened revenge. Yes, sir. And out on the broad Atlantic, where he had followed my daughter in the guise of a sailor, he attempted to murder that child —– my grandchild; but was discovered —–"

"Wait," interrupted the magistrate. "Confine your testimony to the present offense."

"Yes, your Honor. Failing in this, he stole, or enticed the little one from its bed, and in less than five minutes the ship was wrecked, and he must have escaped with the child in ——"

"Were you a witness of this?"

"I was not there, your Honor; but we have it on the word of the first officer, a gentleman ——"

"Step down, sir. That will do. Officer, was this offense committed in New York?"

"Yes, your Honor; I caught him meself."

"Who did be steal the child from?"

"That leddy over yonder."

"Madam, will you take the stand?"

With her child in her arms, Mrs. Selfridge was sworn and in a low, quavering voice repeated what her father had said. Being a woman, she was allowed by the woman—wise magistrate to tell her story in her own way. When she spoke of the attempted murder at the taffrail, her manner became excited. Then she told of the captain's promise to put the man in irons on her agreeing to testify against him —— of the consequent decrease in her watchfulness, and her missing the child just before the shipwreck —— of her rescue by the gallant first officer, and his assertion that he had seen her child in the arms of this man —— the only man on earth who would harm it —— of the later news that a boat containing sailors and children had been picked up by a Mediterranean steamer —— of the detectives sent over, and their report that a sailor answering this man's description had refused to surrender a child to the consul at Gibraltar and had disappeared with it —— of her joy at the news that Myra was alive, and despair of ever seeing her again until she had met her in this man's arms on Broadway the day before. At this point, outraged maternity overcame her. With cheeks flushed, and eyes blazing scorn and anger, she pointed at Rowland and all but screamed: "And he has mutilated —— tortured my baby. There are deep wounds in her little back, and the doctor said, only last night, that they were made by a sharp instrument. And be must have tried to warp and twist the mind of my child, or

52

put her through frightful experiences; for he taught her to swear —— horribly —— and last night at bedtime, when I told her the story of Elisha and the bears and the children, she burst out into the most uncontrollable screaming and sobbing."

Here her testimony ended in a breakdown of hysterics, between sobs of which were frequent admonitions to the child not to say that bad word; for Myra had caught sight of Rowland and was calling his nickname.

"What shipwreck was this —— where was it?" asked the puzzled magistrate of nobody in particular.

"The Titan," called out half a dozen newspaper men across the room.

"The Titan," repeated the magistrate. "Then this offense was committed on the high seas under the English flag. I cannot imagine why it is brought into this court. Prisoner, have you anything to say?"

"Nothing, your Honor." The answer came in a kind of dry sob.

The magistrate scanned the ashen–faced man in rags, and said to the clerk of the court: "Change this charge to vagrancy —— eh ——"

The clerk, instigated by the newspaper men, was at his elbow. He laid a morning paper before him, pointed to certain big letters and retired. Then the business of the court suspended while the court read the news. After a moment or two the magistrate looked up.

"Prisoner," he said, sharply, "take your left sleeve out of your breast!" Rowland obeyed mechanically, and it dangled at his side. The magistrate noticed, and read on. Then he folded the paper and said:

"You are the man who was rescued from an iceberg, are you not?" The prisoner bowed his head.

"Discharged!" The word came forth in an unjudicial roar. "Madam," added the magistrate, with a kindling light in his eye, "this man has merely saved your child's life.

If you will read of his defending it from a polar bear when you go home, I doubt that you will tell it any more bear stories. Sharp instrument —– umph! "Which was equally unjudicial on the part of the court.

Mrs. Selfridge, with a mystified and rather aggrieved expression of face, left the court–room with her indignant father and friends, while Myra shouted profanely for Rowland, who had fallen into the hands of the reporters. They would have entertained him after the manner of the craft, but he would not be entertained —– neither would he talk. He escaped and was swallowed up in the world without; and when the evening papers appeared that day, the events of the trial were all that could be added to the story of the morning.

Chapter Sixteen

ON the morning of the next day, a one–armed dock lounger found an old fish–hook and some pieces of string which he knotted together; then he dug some bait and caught a fish. Being hungry and without fire, he traded with a coaster's cook for a meal, and before night caught two more, one of which he traded, the other, sold. He slept under the docks —– paying no rent —– fished, traded, and sold for a month, then paid for a second–hand suit of clothes and the services of a barber. His changed appearance induced a boss stevedore to hire him tallying cargo, which was more lucrative than fishing, and furnished, in time, a hat, pair of shoes, and an overcoat. He then rented a room and slept in a bed. Before long be found employment addressing envelopes for a mailing firm, at which his fine and rapid penmanship secured him steady work; and in a few months he asked his employers to indorse his application for a Civil Service examination. The favor was granted, the examination easily passed, and he addressed envelopes while he waited. Meanwhile he bought new and better clothing and seemed to have no difficulty in impressing those whom he met with the fact that he was a gentleman. Two years from the time of his examination he was appointed to a lucrative position under the Government, and as he seated himself at the desk in his office, could have been heard to remark: "Now John Rowland, your future is your own. You have merely suffered in the past from a mistaken estimate of the importance of women and whisky."

But he was wrong, for in six months he received a letter which, in part, read as follows:

"Do not think me indifferent or ungrateful. I have watched from a distance while you made your wonderful fight for your old standards. You have won, and I am glad and I congratulate you. But Myra will not let me rest. She asks for you continually and cries at times. I can bear it no longer. Will you not come and see Myra?"

And the man went to see —— Myra.

CPSIA information can be obtained at www.ICGtesting.com
262744BV00003B/44/P

9 781162 664101